Imprint:
© 2016 Elizabeth Kott

English first edition based on the German original translated by the author.
Cover illustration: Elizabeth Kott
Copy editing & setting: Angelika Fleckenstein; spotsrock.de

Publisher: tredition GmbH, Hamburg

Printed in Germany

ISBN: 978-3-7345-2349-6 (Paperback)
       978-3-7345-2350-2 (Hardcover)
       978-3-7345-2351-9 (e-Book)

The work is copyright protected in all its parts. Any use without the consent of the publisher and the author is prohibited. This particularly applies to electronic or other reproduction, translation, distribution and public availability.

Bibliographic information published by the Deutsche Nationalbibliothek (German National Library):
The Deutsche Nationalbibliothek (German National Library) has recorded this publication in the Deutsche Nationalbibliografie (German National Bibliography); detailed bibliographic data are available through the Internet at http://dnb.d-nb.de.

Elizabeth Kott

How a Dolos Became a Dice

Or

Throwing the bones – a journey through time and continents

Table of contents

Preface	7
South Africa	12
The Great Trek	17
Dolos	22
The Etimology	22
The Dutch meaning	22
What the Scientists say	23
1. Afrikaans – English origin	24
2. The Bantu origin	24
3. The Greek or Roman meaning	25
Dolosse as prediction in the rest of the world	31
Europe	31
The game of Dice	32
Playing Dice as lot	36
The first board games	36
Asian historical Dice	36

Predecessor of Backgammon	42
The Distribution by the Romans	44
The origin of Craps – or what might be the origin	44
Other Games of Dice	47
Distribution into the rest of the world	48
Norway	48
Persia (Iran)	50
East Asia	52
China	52
Japan	53
India	54
Mongolia	57
Greece	57
Turkey	59
Dollose as Wave Breakers	60
Literature	62

Preface

As I was producing my book:

> **"Mainzer Hauptfriedhof, ein Spaziergang durch die Gärten der Vergänglichkeit"**,

I came upon a picture of a little girl, throwing dice with knuckle bones.

She had a very contented and dreamy expression, staring into the distance. My husband and I were so impressed by this figurine that he photographed her on various times of the day, in different shades of light. He photographed her with the glaze of the sun falling onto her limbs; he photographed her with snow covering her slim body like a blanket. We were bewitched by this beautiful sculpture and fascinated that she threw dice with knuckle bones, like the children in the Great Trek did in South Africa.

Why does a German Cemetery place this Roman replica on a grave? I immediately exclaimed: "Look, she is throwing dice with "Dolosse". This was the Afrikaans name we used for the knucklebones.

After I finished my book, I was wondering where the figure came from and how it happened that she played her game on a grave in the Main Cemetery of Mainz, in Germany. However, do we know whether it was a game?

In my mother country South Africa we know a similar occurrence, played by Voortrekker children 1838, during the Great Trek, when the Boers tried to flee from the predominance of the British. They organized themselves and travelled with their oxen wagons, all their belongings and their slaves, into the midlands, crossing the Drakensberg, to find new pastures for their cattle and build farms.

The children only had what they found during the breaks. The toys they had were mostly handmade dolls for the girls. The boys had to make their own toys. In the first place they needed lots of phantasy and small objects they could turn into toys with. It happened that they saw that the children of the Natives, who accompanied them, played with knucklebones of sheep or goats and imitated oxen. The jawbones of sheep served as an oxen wagon. The children harnessed their "oxen", in spans of 4 or 6 oxen in front of their "jawbone oxen wagon", although in reality the spans consisted of 16 to 18 oxen.

The original meaning of the knucklebones takes us far back in history. It was not always been meant to be a game, but was also used as prediction by the witch doctor, or medicine man. Much earlier, approximately around 2000 BC the portrayals of people throwing dice with knucklebones were found in caves. Sometimes even the original knucklebones could be found. The habit spread via Egypt and Europe and Asia, almost simultaneously, to be used as prediction by the shaman, and from there on also became known as a game of dice in America and the rest of the world.

I will try to find the context of the different types of games and predictions and present the trip around the world chronologically.

South Africa

The first Europeans to set foot on land were the Portuguese. Bartolomeu Dias anchored 1488 on the southern shore of South Africa. He called it Cape of Storms.

It was later renamed the Cape of Good Hope (Cabo da Boa Esperança) because it represented the opening of a merchant route to the East. During the 16th century, the spice trade was dominated by the Portuguese who used Lisbon as a staple port. The spices, such as cinnamon, cassia, cardamom, ginger, pepper, and turmeric, were supplemented by silk, cotton, porcelain, and textiles. In Batavia the VOC (Dutch East India Company) bought slaves for the later Cape Colony.

However, it was the Dutchman Jan van Riebeeck, accompanied by his wife and son, who set off from Texel in The Netherlands for the Cape of Good Hope. Van Riebeeck had signed a contract with the VOC to oversee the setting up of a refreshment station to supply Dutch ships on their way to the East. Van Riebeeck was accompanied by 82 men and 8 women.

The sailors of the VOC were aboard their ships for a long time. Sometimes six to eight months. Due to a deficiency of vitamin C, they became Scurvy, which at one time was common among sailors aboard ships at sea. Only perishable fruits and vegetables could be stored. Their main foods consisted of cured and salted meats and dried grains. Fruit such as oranges, papaya, strawberries and lemon hardly lasted the long months.

Jan van Riebeeck's aim was to establish a refreshment station to supply the crew of the Company's passing trading ships with fresh water, vegetables and fruit, meat and medical assistance. Van Riebeeck had his strict instructions not to colonize the region but to build a fort and to erect a flagpole to signal ships and boats to escort them into the bay. Although the VOC did not originally intend to establish a colony at the Cape, they finally issued permits. The Cape Colony was erected.

The history of South Africa is characterized by the Great Trek during the 19th Century. More than 12.000 Boers, the so-called "Voortrekkers" left the Cape Colony 1835 with their families and moved North, North-East.

The Great Trek was an eastward and north-eastward emigration away from British control in the Cape Colony during the 1830s and 1840s by the Boers.

Factors causing the Trek included the desire to escape from relentless border wars with the Xhosa along the eastern frontier of the Cape colony. The migrants also sought fertile farmland, as good land was becoming scarce within the colony's frontiers.

Historians have identified various factors though, that contributed to the migration of an estimated 12.000 Voortrekkers to the future Natal, Orange Free State and Transvaal regions.

The primary motivations included discontent with the British rule:

- The Anglicization policies did not offer enough security
- Restrictive laws on slavery and its eventual abolition were one of the main reasons to leave the Cape. This meant that the Whites and Non-Whites (Natives) had an equal status. The first settlers, who came with the VOC, mainly were without their families. These came at a much later stage. It was quite natural for these men to look for women amongst the indigenous Khoisan and Xhosa people, and slaves imported from the Dutch East Indies. This initiated in The Cape Colored's, who resulted from the first settlers. The Colored's are a heterogeneous South African ethnic group, with diverse ancestral links.

- The British authorities were indifferent to border conflicts along the Cape Colony's eastern frontier.

It was quite comfortable for the Boers and their families to keep their slaves and the abolition of slavery caused them to finally start the Great Trek.

The Great Trek

The main intention of the Voortrekker was to obtain fertile farmland in Natal.

As a means of transport for their trek into the Interior they used oxen wagons. For a long time this was their only homestead.

In the resting phases, or during battles with the Zulu, the oxen wagons were pulled into a laager. A laager, also known as a wagon fort, was a mobile fortification made of wagons arranged into a rectangle, a circle or other shape and possibly joined with each other, an improvised military camp. This served as protection for man and beast.

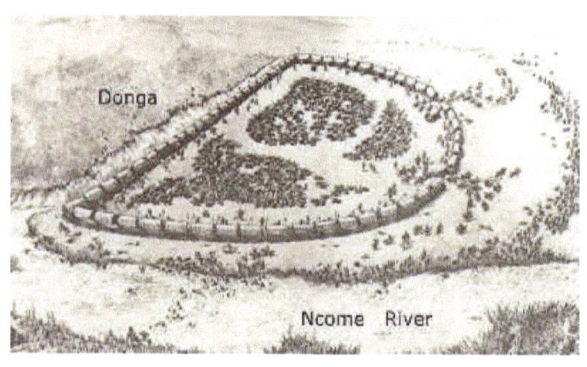

In this laager the children played and preparations were made for the expected battles. The women and girls were responsible for preparing meals, baking bread in termite hills, or keeping the clothing up to date. However, they were also responsible for pouring lead for ammunition and keeping it in store.

From early childhood onwards, the boys were trained to handle life with all its dangers and hardships. They had to help their elders to protect the laager. Already as a toddler, they had to learn to ride on horseback and learn to shoot. This meant that they had to handle the heavy muzzle-loaders, which were eminent for surviving.

Children were begot and born in the wagons, and they grew up knowing nothing but the trek-wagon.

In spite of all the dangers, the Voortrekker children still found time to play. Mostly, they imitated the habits of the adults. Sometimes, in the areas where clay was found in abundance, the boys built real wagons and the girls had to sew the canvas planes. Otherwise they used knucklebones of sheep or goats. Leather thongs were fastened to sticks to make a long whip, as used by the native driver to spur on the oxen. The boys then spanned them in, in front of jaw bones with these leather reams. As in reality each ox had his special name, such as Kraalman, Zoeloe, Voorslag, Boesman or Rooiman.

The trek-wagon was drawn by a span of sixteen oxen.

The wagons moved at walking speed during the morning, rested at midday and covered a few more miles before evening. They were packed both with rough furniture, family heirlooms, farming equipment, seeds, coffee, sugar, gunpowder and other necessities. Hanging underneath were cages of chickens.

The animals called for would one by one step out of the crowd and come to stand in their allotted positions Not only would the driver – 'u shangele' – know each ox by name, but the performance of his team would have vastly to do with his ability to walk alongside them, flicking his whip just above their ears. (It was considered bad technique, by the way, to make the whip actually descend on the animal.) and cajoling them like so many individuals. Talking to his animals, the driver might, over a period of two or three weeks, walk from Pietermaritzburg, say, to Salisbury in the new-found Rhodesia, now Simbabwe.

Given the great weight of the wagon behind them, it was a matter of principle to select the two most massive, best-tempered animals as the after-pair, the ones who would be attached to the disselboom itself. These great creatures could send the message 'brake required' all the way along the span by the solid application of their own braking force.

(Unsung heroes: the trek ox and Natal)

Dolos

The Etimology

The etymological meaning of the Afrikaans word "Dolos", meaning the knucklebones of sheep or goats probably derives from Dutch. However, up till now it is still not completely clear where the word originated from.

The Dutch meaning

A possible meaning could be the contraction from "dobbel-osse", double oxen. The oxen were spanned-in in pairs i.e. "double". It is more likely however, that the word originates from the Dutch word "Dobbeloosie". The knucklebone is also called "oosbeentjie" which is used as dice, or for divination. "Dobbel" also indicates that the knucklebone was used as a dice. In Afrikaans the word "dobbel" also means throwing dice, gambling. The form of the knucklebone was crucial for the later games of dice.

The dolos was mainly used by the Sangoma – a South African witch doctor. He takes a handful of knuckle bones, sometimes together with pieces of wood or even shells to predict the future. When you ask the Sangoma something he takes the knucklebones in both hands. Then he throws them onto the ground, or the skin of an antelope, or onto a grass mat. According to the position of the throw he can interpret the answer.

What the Scientists say

1. *Afrikaans – English origin*

In the dissertation of G.S. Nienaber (South African Journal of Linguistics; suppl. 23 – ISSN 1018-7820) **DIE ETIMOLOGIE VAN DOLOS,** I would like to quote several passages:

Rev. Noel Roberts (1916:400) says:

"In South Africa the Boers call them "dol-ossen", or toy oxen, and this word has been retained in the phrase "dolossen gooi" (throw the dolosse)

Rev. Roberts sees the word "dol" as an equivalent of the English "doll", meaning toy. Herewith he derives the name from **Afrikaans-English**.

2. *The Bantu origin*

Prof. S.P.E. Boshoff claims in his dissertation (1921), via a quotation from Theal:

"If an ox strayed, the daula was thrown to ascertain in what direction it had gone. If a hunt was to take place, it was consulted to indicate in what quarter game was most readily to be found. In short it was resorted to in every case of doubt."

His explanation of the etymological meaning is that the native word "daula" is the origin of "dolos", i.e. originating from **Bantoid meanings**. Both indicating the toy of the boys, as well as the divination, when the witchdoctor throws the knucklebones with both hands, mumbling his spell.

F.J. Lategan (1987) also refers to the possibility that the word "dolos" is derived from Zulu or Xhosa languages. In Xhosa "Idolo" means knee or ankle. Also found in "u-dolo" or "dolosi", meaning dice.

3. *The Greek or Roman meaning*

The scientific name is Greek (astralogos), or Latin (talus).

It is very improbable however, that the Afrikaans word "dolos" was derived from Latin, although it sounds very similar: "talos" or "dolos", as the Afrikaans children did not know Latin or Greek.

There are thus three indications for the word "Dolos".

1. The first indication is the toy the boys play with. Either as clay oxen, or as the knucklebone of sheep or goats.
2. The second indication is predicting the future, or diagnosing illness. The position, in which the "dolos" falls, indicates the reading.

J.H. Albert Kropf in "A Kafir-English Dictionary (1899, Lovedale") mentions:

"Bones of different animals used by witch doctors as dice to foretell the fortune or misfortune of man or a party."

Rev. N. Roberts gives us a description of the way the oracle is read:

- *Certain roots are chewed by the diviner*

- *The astragli are gathered up between the palms of the two hands.*

- *The deviner blows or spits upon them, and utters a short incantation or formula calling upon the "bones" to reveal the answer to the question given.*

- *The "bones" are then cast upon the ground before the squatting seer, and an answer gleaned from the position they assume"*

To give more precise information I will describe the way the witchdoctor works.

The prediction is as follows:

In bone divination, bones of various sorts are ritually tossed onto a mat, an animal hide, or into a circle drawn in the dirt, and the resulting patterns interpreted. Throwing the bones is an ancient practice traditional to many regions of the world, including Africa, Asia, and North America. The number and type of bones employed, as well as the inclusion of other small objects, such as pebbles, shells, and hard nuts, varies quite a bit from culture to culture. The practice is called "throwing the bones."

The Sangoma takes the knucklebones or „Dolosse" from a bag, made of springbuck hide. Each tribe has their own specific kind of "dolosse". It could be combined by a couple of shells, eight holy pebbles (four of wood and four of ivory). Two of each sort of knucklebones, according to gender. Even pebbles out of the stomach of crocodiles, or parts of turtles could be amongst the "dolosse". After his patient or client takes place in front of him on the ground, he takes a mat, which may only be used for throwing the bones.

The patient then has to blow into the bag of springbuck hide. The Sangoma closes his eyes and concentrates. Then he throws the bones three times, whilst mumbling a monotone spell. His wide range of knowledge of herbs and ointments enables the Sangoma to prepare a medicine (Muti) for his patient. The "Dolosse" then answer the questions the patient asked him. Throwing the dice gives directives for all situations in life.

Throwing the bones (impamba) is practiced in different African cultures. Mainly meant as divination, but also used as a method of diagnosing and curing illness. It is unknown where the divination originated from as already since thousands of years, throughout the world the shaman practiced it. In southern Africa the first recording about "astragali" as the knucklebones are also called, used as oracle or prediction, was made by the Portuguese missionary Joana dos Santos in 1607.

3. The third indication is completely different from the two other ones. Here it is meant as a wave breaker. At the end of this book, the explanation of the dolos, as wave breaker is given.

Branford and Brandford (1991, 4th edition p. 81) quote-:

"Formerly known as Merrifield blocks: interlocking concrete blocks called by the inventor "dolosse", used all over the world to preserve beaches and harbours from being washed away."

"They look like concrete jigsaw puzzles dumped on the beach. They are called dolosse and are the brainchild of Mr. E.M. Merrifield, East London's harbor engineer. Star 10.4.73"

"Hong Kong Reservoir reinforced with nearly 7000 dolosse, each weighing twenty-five tons and shaped like a giant letter H with one arm twisted through 90°. This effectively dissipate the force of the breakers. Illustrated London News Nov. 1976"

Dolosse as prediction in the rest of the world

Europe

In the Greek and Roman culture the knucklebones, called "Astragali" were used to predict the future. Due to their edged shapes there were four different possible positions in which they fell and in which the prediction lay. Already the antique authors had their theories about the origin. Plinius the elder e.g. ascribed it to be Palamedes under the Trojan War, as well as Herodot from the Lydian People. The Lydians were an Indo-European volk, living in the western area of Asia-minor.

It is assumed, however, that the origin lies in the Orient. Already six-edged dice, as well as higher edged numbers were known. A wide spectrum of other materials than knucklebones are known, such as clay, metal, ivory, crystal bones and glass. It even existed dice with letters and words instead of numbers and eyes. These were used for divination or more complexed games of dice.

The game of Dice

There were two game modes in Antiquity. The first one, and probably the most primitive method, was throwing the knucklebones into the air and catching them on the back of your hand. Even today it is still played in the same way, but nowadays with dice. This easy method was usually played by women and girls and was called "pent alit ha", or five dice. This game was played in different variations.

One of these variations was called "Tropa" or "Game in the hole". In this game the player had to throw the bones into a hole in the ground. The other variation from the original game was a game of hazard. The bones had to be thrown onto a table, either by hand, or also from a mug. The numbers of the edges on which it fell were counted.

In this game the form and type of knucklebone characterized the manner of counting. The knucklebones of sheep or goats have two rounded edges, on which it could not land, as well as two wide and two thin edges, one concave and one convex.

In the Roman Empire throwing dice and Astragli, used for gambling for money, was forbidden, except on the Saturnalia. This was a Roman holiday in honor of the God Saturn, who was seen as the Ruler of the primeval golden age.

Tacitus mentions the passion of the Germane for gambling in his "Germania". According to Tacitus they played in rational state with utter carelessness, risking everything, even their own freedom. During the Middle Ages "throwing dice" was the favorite preoccupation of the knights. Even schools for playing dice and guilds were erected. After the fall of Feudalism the "Landsknechte" got the reputation of being notorious dice players.

Max Kaltenmoser 1842-1887

The pastime with the probability of getting addicted was forbidden in the Middle Ages. In 1396 in Mailand, Italy, a person not adhering to the law was fined 200 Lire and had to remove himself at least 100 miles from the city.

Playing Dice as lot

There are many biblical references to lots, e.g. Psalm 22. There it is described that they cast lots for a garment. This was common practice in the region during the reign of King David. The choices that were common, were names, or times written on a piece of wood or clay. These lots were then put into a jar or piece of clothing and jogged around, until one appears. This way it was a fair form of selection.

The first board games

Asian historical Dice

The eldest known dice belongs to an old Iranian board game, dated 5000 BC. This was probably the predecessor of Backgammon. Further early findings were made in Tepe Gawra (Northern Iraq), early 3rd Century, as well as Mohenijo-Daro (Pakistan) in the late 3rd. Century. These findings already had the form of a cube and were designed with eyes.

In the early history and Antique of the Orient many six-edged dice were maintained.

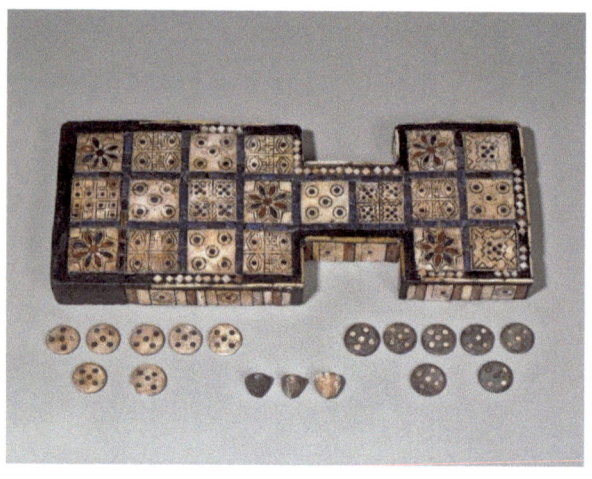

The Royal Game of Ur, also known as the Game of Twenty Squares, refers to an ancient game represented by two game boards found in the Royal Tombs of Ur in Iraq by Sir Leonard Woolley in the 1920s. The two boards date from the First Dynasty of Ur, before 2600 BC, thus making the Royal Game of Ur one of the oldest examples of board gaming equipment found, although Senet boards found in Egyptian graves predate it as much as 900 years. The Ur-style Twenty Squares game board was also known in Egypt as Asseb, and has been found in Pharaoh Tutankhamen's tomb, among other places. The oldest known form of this game is shown in a painting in the tomb of Hesy (approx. 2686-2613 BC)

A graffito version of the game was discovered on one of the human-headed winged bull gate sentinels from the palace of Sargon II (721–705 BC) in the city of Khorsabad now in the British Museum in London (see illustration). Similar games have since been discovered on other sculptures in other museums.

A version of the game exists until today in the Jewish population of Knochi, a city in the South of India.

Egyptian aristocrats of 3,500 years ago passed the time with a backgammon-like tabletop game, Spanish archaeologists have discovered. Jose Manuel Galan and his team made the discovery at Luxor.

(Wikipedia - Scientists discover Egyptians' 'backgammon' Expatica [Netherlands], 6 April 2006)
Proyecto Djehuty

The collection of marble pieces for the game, known as "senet," was found in the ancient Egyptian capital, inside a mound holding the tombs of XVIII dynasty nobles Djehuty and Hery. Galan and his team found the senet pieces 2006.

More than 40 board games with knucklebones were found in the graves of Ancient Egypt. The archaic Senet games were discovered carved into the rock ledges. It is assumed that the pyramid workers played during their resting times. The first knuckle bones were already found during the 1st Dynasty and the boards in the 3rd Dynasty. This game belongs to the earliest board games.

Predecessor of Backgammon

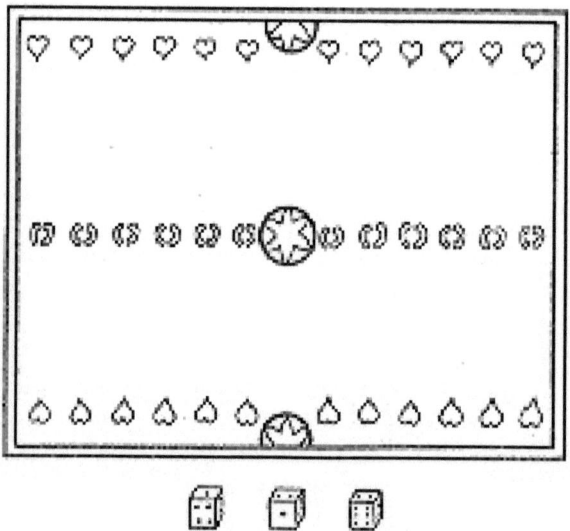

The ancient Romans played a number of games, surprisingly identical to Backgammon. The game of 12 lines (see picture), also called "The lines of twelve philosophers".

This game was played all across the Roman Empire, in taverns, brothels, private homes and frontier forts. Numerous boards have been found from Egypt to Britain, but especially in and around Rome. Although this game appears to be the same as Duodecim Scripta, the matter is not entirely clear. These particular gaming boards contained six words or six letters.

Many experts believe this game is actually a version of the Greek game Diagramismos. In this form, it bears a strong resemblance to Egyptian Senet, which had 30 squares. Since gambling was banned in Rome, it would appear that the words simply disguised the board.

Also called Tabula (Byzantine Greek: τάβλη), meaning a plank or board was a Greco-Roman board game, and is generally thought to be the direct ancestor of modern backgammon. The earliest description of "τάβλη" (tavli) is in an epigram of Byzantine emperor Zeno given by Agathias of Myrine (6th century AD) in which the game is similarly played as Backgammon.

The Distribution by the Romans

It was the Roman legionnaires and settlers, as well as the Arabs who brought the game with Astragali or knuckle bones to the rest of Europe. Although the Romans spread the game, it was also found in countries where the Romans never were, from Russia to Polynesia.

It was e.g. also a game played in Iran by the Kurds.

During the Middle Ages the knucklebones were called humpback horns, but gradually regularly shaped dice were used exclusively. As already used in the Antique, six-sided dice were dominant.

There were different ways of playing the game. Some threw the Astragali, but others played more a game of skill, in which many different figures had to be thrown.

The Romans and the Arabs spread the game with astragali to Europe. Thus a game was born, that until our time is still very popular and is called "Craps".

The origin of Craps – or what might be the origin

In the Arabic language dice are called "az-zahr", from which the expression "game of hazard" originated. Games played with dice were considered as gambling per se and already played by the Chinese and soldiers of the Roman Empire.

Craps developed from a simplification of the early English game of "hazard". Its origins are complex and may date to the Crusades, later being influenced by French gamblers. What was to become the modern American version of the game was brought to New Orleans by Bernard Xavier Philippe de Marigny de Mandeville, a gambler and politician descended from wealthy Louisiana landowners.

As far as the evolution of craps into the game it is today, according to some, can be traced to the Crusades, 1125 A.D. Specifically when English soldiers, including most notably Sir William Tyre, started to play it in the process of seizing an Arabian castle that was called "Hazart." Whether the Arabian influence was anywhere to be found in their adoption of the game is not clear. What is known is that the English latched on to the game and it became known as "Hazard" in 1550.

1700 Craps crossed the Atlantic into the French Colony Arcadia, Nova Scotia, nowadays called Canada.

1755 the Colony belonged to the British Empire, who banned the French speaking inhabitants. In their despair they fled and found a new home in Louisiana.

Named the Cajuns, these people brought with them a language of their own and a rich culture; part of this culture was the dice game of crabs, which they referred to as "crebs" or "creps".

The game, first known as "crapaud" (a French word meaning "toad" in reference to the original style of play by people crouched over a floor or sidewalk), reportedly owes its modern popularity to street craps. Street craps may be played by rolling the dice against a back-stop, such as a curb or stair-stoop, or without a back-stop, at the choice of the players. During World War II, street-style craps became popular among soldiers, who often played it using an Army blanket as a shooting surface

Until now it is still argued about the time and place where the game of Craps originated from.

There are some that argue that Craps came to America along with the first English settlers on the Mayflower. It is quite possible that Craps spread from both the English and the French, each one bringing their own version of the game. Due to the popularity of the dice usage of Craps, the basics of the game always remained the same.

The tables used by Craps players are very large and attract quite a number of people. They can therefore easily be found in casinos.

In British casinos, around 1800 there were special people who swallowed the dice, in case of police raids. Dice games were forbidden.

Other experts claim that Craps already existed during the Holy Roman Empire. The Roman Legion soldiers prepared dice from pig knuckles. This was their possibility of resting between battles.

Other Games of Dice

In France they played a game called Passe-dix, also called "passage" in English. It is a game of chance using dice. Passe-dix is one of the, possibly the, most ancient of all games of chance, and is said to have actually been made use of by the executioners at the crucifixion of our Saviour, when they parted his garments, casting lots, Matt. xxvii. 35.

Distribution into the rest of the world

It is very difficult to give a chronological distribution of the games, played with knucklebones or dice, as they spread through the world.

Norway

Viking Gaming and Gambling
Published by Morten on Mon, 24/03/2014 - 15:06
"There is plenty of archaeological evidence that Vikings enjoyed dice games, sets of hand carved dice have been found at burial sites across Scandinavia and the British Isles, these dice were used in board games, but also on their own in a game called "Mia" or "Liar Dice." Mia was a dice game that because of its bluffing element was in some ways similar to poker."

The dice the Vikings played with were made of fish bones, antlers, bone or cole.

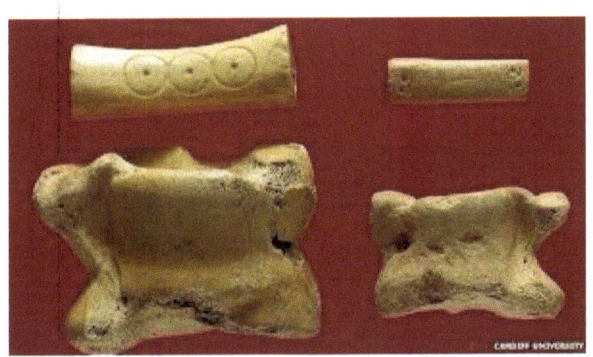

Dice originating approx. 680 BC

Persia (Iran)

Nard (game)

The game has been historically popular in Persia, Muslim countries, and among Babylonian Jews. The name nardshir comes from the Persian nard (Wooden block) and shir (lion) referring to the two type of pieces used in play.

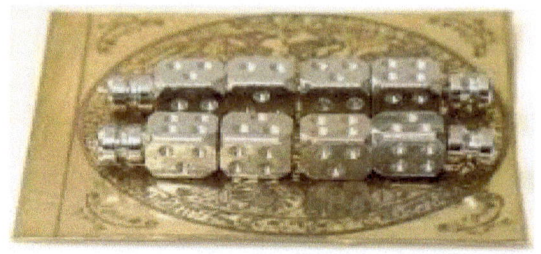

The oldest known dice originates about 5000 years ago, from the region of present Iran. They were four-sided knuckle bones from sheep or goats.

 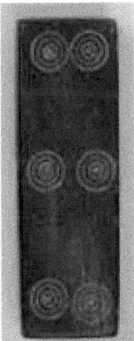

A common legend associates the game with the founder of the Sassanian dynasty, Ardshir. The oldest known reference to the game is thought to be a passage in the Talmud, although some claim it refers to the Greek game Kubeia. Another early reference is to be found in the Middle Persian romance of Chatrang-namak (written between the 7th and 9th centuries) which attributes the invention of the game to Bozorgmehr.

By the 17th century the game was played in Georgia under the name of nardi, and by the 19th century it was being played by the Kalmucks (who called it narr). During most part of the 20th century both Georgia and Kalmucks were parts of USSR, so now the game is played in Russia and other ex-USSR countries under the name of nardy.

Excavations at Shahr-e Sukhteh (Persian literally "The Burnt City") in Iran have shown that a board race game existed there around 3000 BC. The artifacts include two dice and 60 checkers, and the set is believed to be 100 to 200 years older than the Royal Game of Ur. On the board found at Shahr-e Sukhteh the fields are fashioned by the coils of a snake.

East Asia

China

Backgammon was popular in China for a time and was known as "shuanglu" with the book Pǔ Shuāng) written during the Southern Song (1127–1279) period recording over ten variants.

Japan

In Japan ban-sugoroku is thought to have been introduced from China in the sixth century. As a gambling game it was made illegal several times. In the early Edo-era, a new and quick gambling game called

Chō-han appeared and sugoroku quickly dwindled. By the 13th century the board game Go, originally played only by the aristocracy, had become popular among the general public.

India

In ancient India, people were using cubic dice by the Harappan period, about 2000 BC. Sometimes people also used stick dice, like flattened toothpicks, which only have four sides. And sometimes they threw groups of cowrie shells, and your score depended on how many shells landed with their teeth facing up.

In the Dice Game in Old India from the essay of Heinrich Lüders "Das Würfelspiel im alten Indien, Berlin, 1906" Lüders says:

"Dice Games

A major difficulty in comprehending the dice game is that there are different sorts of dice and different types of games that are talked of in the same words.

Another difficulty is that the commentators tend to describe the type of game entering into the details. The main stress will be laid on the dice game in the Mahæbhærata.

Dice

Under the generic term akÒa, very different types of dice are to be found. I will review them:

Vibhitaka Nuts:

The fruits of the Vibhitaka tree, the size of a hazelnut, were called "the browns, babhru" in the Veda. They were the dice used in the oldest periods, from the Vedic to the ritual and the epic dice games

Cauri Shells, (kaparda, kapardaka) could have played the same role as the vibhitaka nuts. They could also have been played by counting those which fall the rounded side upside or downside.

Pæaka (or pæa):

Right prisms, about 7 x 1 x 1 cm for some, sometimes in gold or in any other matter, sometimes coloured. The four long sides are marked with dots (eyes, akÒas), generally from 1 to 4. In certain games played with three pæakas, each one is marked with a special sign. pæakas seems not to have been known in Vedic times.

In the texts of Bhartṛhari also romanised as Bhartrihari; fl. c. 5th century CE) who is a Sanskrit author, it is assumed due to his mentioning of playing dice in his "Vairagya-satakam", that maybe the origin of dice games lies in India."

Mongolia

Other archaeological excavations from the old graves in the Indus-Tal civilization point to an East Asian origin.

The modern Mongoles still use a game played with knuckle bones in their game "Shagai". This game also serves for divination.

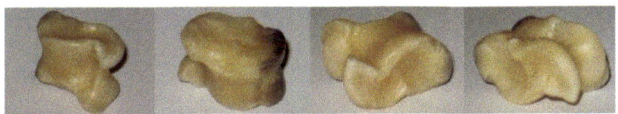

Greece

Backgammon is popular among modern Greeks until now. It is a game in which Greeks usually tease their opponent and they create a lively atmosphere. The game is called "Tavli", derived in Byzantine times from the Latin word "tabula. A game, almost identical to backgammon, called Tavli (Byzantine Greek: τάβλη) is described in an epigram of the Byzantine Emperor Zeno (AD 476–481).[41

Turkey

Backgammon, which is known as "tavla," from Byzantine Greek τάβλη is also still a very popular game in Turkey, and it is customary to name the dice rolls with their Persian number names: yek (1), dü (2), se (3), cehar (4), penc (5), şeş (6).

There are many variants of tavla in Turkey, where the course of play changes drastically. The usual tavla is also known as erkek tavlası meaning boys' or men's tavla. The other variant kız tavlası (meaning girls' tavla) is a game that depends only on the dice and involves no strategy. There is another variant called asker tavlası (meaning soldiers' tavla) where the pieces are thrown to the board randomly and the opponents try to flip their pieces over the opponents' pieces to beat them.

The usual Tavla rules are the same as in the other neighboring Arab countries and Greece, as established over a millennium ago.

Dollose as Wave Breakers

How a child's game with knucklebones became one of the largest inventions worldwide, is an interesting story and again takes us to South Africa, where we started.

The wave breakers, called "Dolosse" are curiously formed concrete blocks, looking like ankles. They are used to break the waves along the shore and are implemented worldwide a thousand times, as protection against storms. The early seafarer initially called the most southern point of South Africa the Cape of Storms. Enormous storms whipped ashore and caused great damage. 1963 such a storm fell on the Eastern Cape and destroyed large parts of the country. At this time Eric Merrifield and Audry Kruger were harbor engineers in the city of East London. It was their job to find a solution to prevent the damage caused by the storms. The solution had to be inexpensive and not require great precision and know-how. During his lunch break Audry Kruger went home and modelled out of pieces of broom handle the solution. He nailed the pieces together, shaping an "H"and turning one leg in 90°. The invention of the "Dolos" was made. This model was poured into concrete. As Kruger and Merrifield tested their invention, they threw smaller models into the air, to see how the parts would fall together, and mingle with each other, Kruger's father joined them an and commented laconically in Afrikaans:

"Ah, are you playing with dolosse?"
This was the birth of the name!

Literature

The Trek Wagon
The Great Trek of the Voortrekkers
Durban Website Designers
Gedagtes vir elke dag
Die Jongspan – Kleiosse

http://www.Gelofteland.org
Die Suidafrikaanse Jeug in Voortrekkertydperk
J.A. Visser

Scientia Militaria, South African Journal of Military Studies, Vol. 15, Nr. 3, 1985

Dolosse, Ossewaens and my Brother Les

Blog of Vernon Whittal, 27.2.2011
Bones throwing Witchdoctors: A Day in the Other Africa
http://www.oldsoulsgathering.com

Die Etimologie van dolos
G.S.Nienaber
South African Journal of Linguistics, Supplement
23, February 1995

Great South African Inventions
Mike Bruton

African Branch Educators News

Cronicles the West Coast of South Africa

Marie Theron
Spiele und Spielzeug in der Antike

Marco Fitta
Auxilior@imperiumromanum.com
Gesellschaftsspiele der Römer – Astragaloi
Spielen mit Astragalen
Ulrich Schädler
    Archäologischer Anzeiger 1, 1996, S. 61-73 124

Other German Books by the Author:

Acht Monate unseres Lebens im afrikanischen Busch, 2. Auflage 2014, tredition Verlag Hamburg
978-3-8495-7746-9 (Hardcover)
978-3-8495-7775-9 (Paperback)
978-3-8495-7747-6 (eBook)

Waterfalls eine Farm in Südafrika, Verlorene Heimat – Abenteuer in der Türkei, 2014 tredition Verlag Hamburg
978-3-8495-5146-9 (Paperback)
978-3-7323-0070-9 (eBook)

Fiepie und Konsorten …und viele ganz andere Katzengeschichten, 2015 tredition Verlag Hamburg
978-3-7323-2991-5 (Paperback)
978-3-7323-2992-2 (Hardcover)
978-3-7323-2993-9 (eBook)

Kater Johnnys Krimi oder Herbert Simmerings Machenschaften, 2015 tredition Verlag Hamburg
978-3-7323-5847-2 (Paperback)
978-3-7323-5848-9 (Hardcover)
978-3-7323-6133-5 (eBook)